JENNY'S JOURNEY

Library of Congress Cataloging in Publication Data

Saito, Michiko, 1946—
   Jenny's journey.

   SUMMARY: Jenny and her cat, Shoe, pack a picnic
basket and set off on a hike into the forest at the
edge of town where they encounter some unexpected
things.
   I. Title.
PZ7.S14393Je |E| 74-2086
ISBN 0-07-054461-1
ISBN 0-07-054462-X (lib. bdg.)

JENNY'S JOURNEY

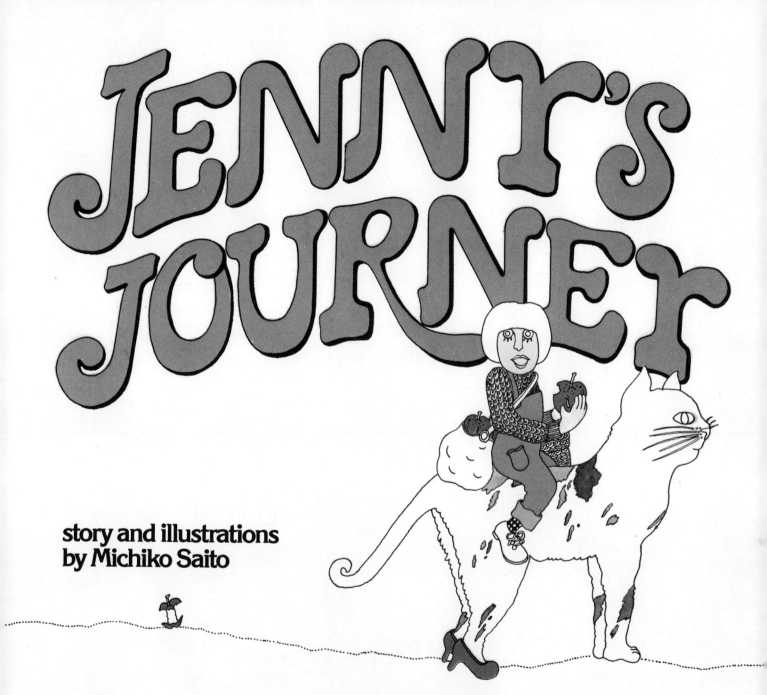

story and illustrations by Michiko Saito

McGraw-Hill Book Company

New York St. Louis San Francisco Düsseldorf Johannesburg
Kuala Lumpur London Mexico Montreal New Delhi Panama
Rio de Janeiro Singapore Sydney Toronto

DEDICATED
TO
LEIGH DEAN
WITHOUT WHOM
JENNY WOULD
NEVER HAVE
STARTED FOR
A JOURNEY

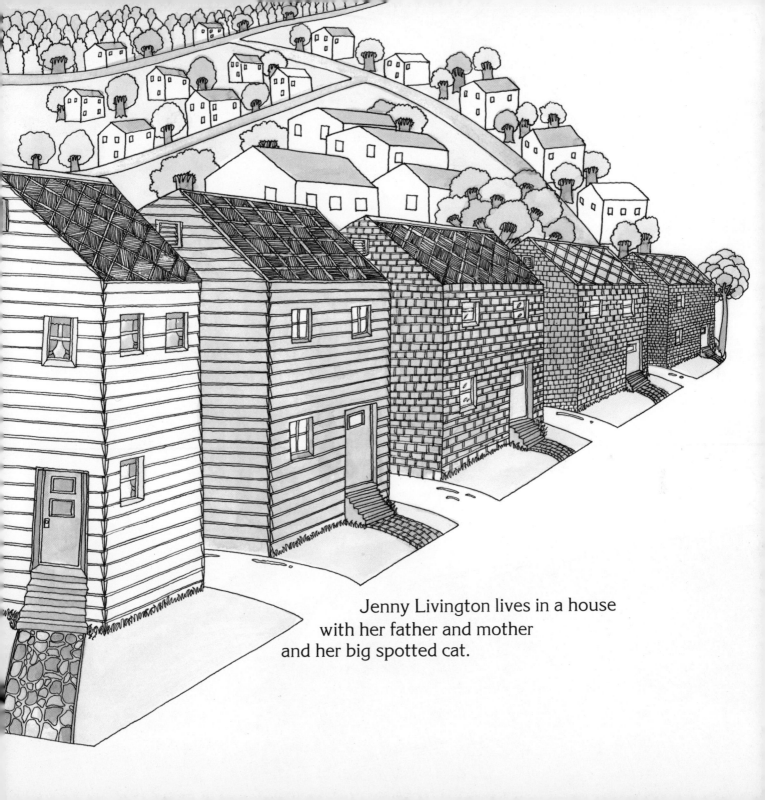

Jenny Livington lives in a house
with her father and mother
and her big spotted cat.

The cat is called Shoe
because she likes to wear
Mrs. Livington's old
red shoes. Mrs. Livington
gives them to Shoe
when she buys new red ones.

One sunny morning, Jenny asked her mother
if she could go for a hike with Shoe.

"There's a forest at the edge of town.
I want to see what it's like," said Jenny.

"All right," said her mother. "But you
must come home before dark."

Mother made peanut butter sandwiches for Jenny
and a tuna fish salad for Shoe. She also gave them
a basket full of apples, which were Jenny's
favorite fruit.

"Get on my back," said Shoe.

"Here we go," said Jenny.

"Have a nice time," said mother.

They left town and soon they were in the woods.

"It's so beautiful," shouted Jenny,
getting off Shoe's back.

"Smells green and chewy," said Shoe,
stretching herself against a tree.

Singing, dancing, and
picking flowers, they went
deep into the woods.

They were taking a rest in the grass
when they saw two rabbits.

"Hi," said Jenny and Shoe.

"Hello," said the two rabbits. "What are you doing?"

"We are hiking," said Jenny. "We came from town."

"Did you really," said the rabbits. "We are going
to the most beautiful place in the forest. It is
called Flower Garden. Would you like to join us?"

"Yes," said Jenny and Shoe.

The two rabbits led the way.

Flower Garden was
filled with flowers.
And they were in full bloom.

In the middle of Flower Garden,
there was a pond.
Jenny and Shoe and the two rabbits
met some ducks there.

"The bears are giving a rock concert
in the forest square," said the ducks.

"Let's go," said the rabbits.

Everyone hurried to the square.

The ducks led the way.

They arrived just in time
to hear the bears tuning up.
The audience clapped and sang
while the bears played tunes
from their hit records.

After the concert, Jenny Livington opened the picnic basket and invited everyone to have a snack. They were all having a great time eating and chatting— when suddenly...

...a bird landed on the branch of a broken tree. He looked very upset.

"We need help!" shouted the bird. "Woodcutters cut down many trees this morning and our nests crashed to the ground. Many baby birds fell with the nests and they are hurt. I was sent to get help. Please, come! Hurry!"

Everybody wanted to help. But, as they hurried after

the bird, there was a sudden raining of acorns.

Suddenly, the raining stopped. Many squirrels ran down from the trees.

"Welcome to our land," said the squirrels.

"We are in a hurry," said Jenny.

"Where are you going?" asked the squirrels.

"We are hurrying to help some poor birds whose trees got chopped down this morning," explained Jenny.

"That's awful," said the squirrels. "We will come along and help the birds, too."

The monkeys even made themselves
into a bridge to make a shortcut
over a rushing river.

"Please, hurry," called the bird,
leading the way.

Everybody hurried.

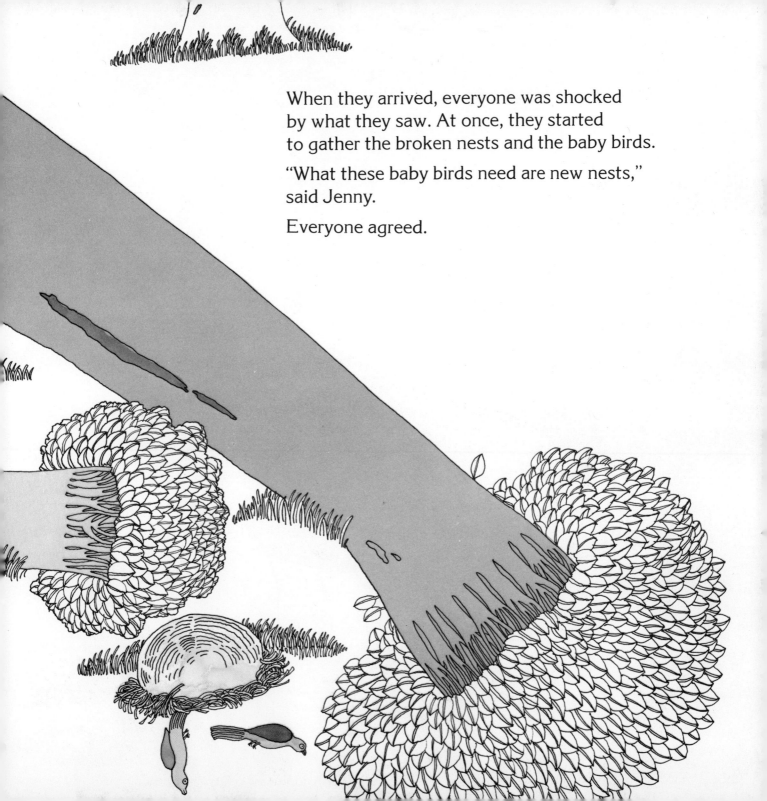

When they arrived, everyone was shocked
by what they saw. At once, they started
to gather the broken nests and the baby birds.

"What these baby birds need are new nests,"
said Jenny.

Everyone agreed.

The squirrels got busy and carved six
new bird homes in a long piece of wood.

The ducks found an empty nutshell and filled it with dry grass to make a nice, soft nest.

One of the rabbits even
stood on his hands
to cheer up the baby birds,

while the bears used a
bandanna and their hippy
headbands and made a
swinging birdhouse.

Shoe gave her pair of red shoes,
Jenny donated her picnic basket,
and the monkeys discussed how and
where they should place the new nests.

The woodcutters had left one tall, aged tree standing. The monkeys decided to hang the nests there.

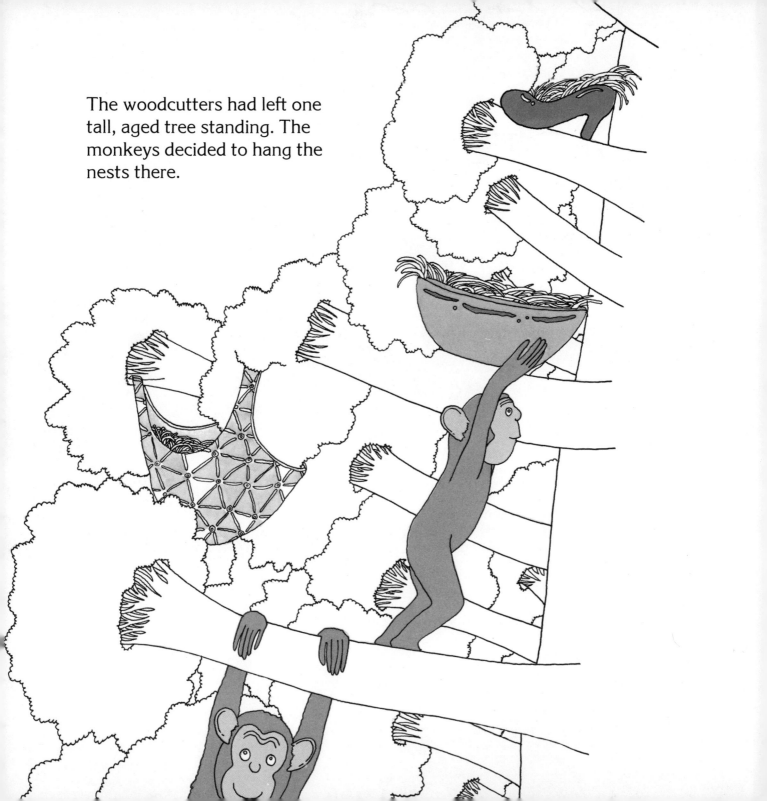

The job was finally done.
The birds were happy and thankful.

As Jenny and Shoe were about to
leave, two birds came flying from
the tree. They carried two pairs
of vine-leaf shoes for Shoe and a
special leafy gift for Jenny.

Now the sun was sinking low
and it was time for Jenny
and Shoe to go home.
Rabbits, ducks, bears, monkeys,
squirrels, and birds came to the
edge of the forest to see them off.

"Good-bye," said the animals.

"Good-bye," said Jenny and Shoe.

"We had a wonderful time. Thank you all."

"Come and see us again," said the animals.

And everyone waved good-bye.

"Hello," said mother.

"Hello," said father, when Jenny and Shoe got home.

"Did you have a nice time?" they asked.

"Oh, yes," said Jenny.

"Oh, yes," purred Shoe.